Jam

Plum Jam

4 lbs of stoned plums
4 lbs of sugar
½ a pint of water.

Simmer the plums
in the water until
soft. Add the sugar
and stir until
dissolved. Boil
until the jam will
set.
Put into clean warm
jars and seal well.

PUFFIN BOOKS
Published by the Penguin Group
Penguin Group (NZ), 67 Apollo Drive, Rosedale,
North Shore 0632, New Zealand (a division of Pearson New Zealand Ltd)
Penguin Group (USA) Inc., 375 Hudson Street,
New York, New York 10014, USA
Penguin Group (Canada), 90 Eglinton Avenue East, Suite 700, Toronto,
Ontario, M4P 2Y3, Canada (a division of Pearson Penguin Canada Inc.)
Penguin Books Ltd, 80 Strand, London, WC2R 0RL, England
Penguin Ireland, 25 St Stephen's Green,
Dublin 2, Ireland (a division of Penguin Books Ltd)
Penguin Group (Australia), 250 Camberwell Road, Camberwell,
Victoria 3124, Australia (a division of Pearson Australia Group Pty Ltd)
Penguin Books India Pvt Ltd, 11, Community Centre,
Panchsheel Park, New Delhi – 110 017, India
Penguin Books (South Africa) (Pty) Ltd, 24 Sturdee Avenue,
Rosebank, Johannesburg 2196, South Africa

Penguin Books Ltd, Registered Offices: 80 Strand, London, WC2R 0RL, England

First published by J. M. Dent & Sons Ltd, 1985
Published in Puffin Books, 1996
This edition published in Puffin Books, 2010
10 9 8 7 6 5 4 3

Copyright © Margaret Mahy, 1985
Illustrations © Helen Craig, 1985

The right of Margaret Mahy to be identified as the author of this work in terms of
section 96 of the Copyright Act 1994 is hereby asserted.

Designed by Book Design Ltd www.bookdesign.co.nz
Printed in China through Asia Pacific Offset Ltd, Hong Kong

ISBN: 9 78 0 14350439 9

A catalogue record for this book is available
from the National Library of New Zealand.

www.penguin.co.nz

Jam

Written by Margaret Mahy

Illustrated by Helen Craig

PUFFIN BOOKS

Mr and Mrs Castle lived in a white house with a big green lawn. Their three children were called Clement, Clarissa and Carlo.

'Three little Castles,' said Mr Castle, 'but very small ones – more like Cottages, really.'

Mrs Castle was the cleverest Castle of the whole family.

'What a one *she* is,' said Mr Castle. 'She could whip up a pot of atomic porridge. She could tuck a computer into bed and sing it to sleep with a lullaby. If she decided to go to the moon I don't think she'd even need a rocket to get there.' He was very proud of his wife.

One day Mrs Castle announced that she had found herself a job. Important scientists were developing an electronic medicine to cure sunspots and they had sent for Mrs Castle.

'But who is going to look after us?' asked Clement.

'Isn't anyone going to be here when we come home from school?' asked Clarissa. Carlo was too young to say anything, but he also looked worried.

'*I* shall be here, my dear little Cottages,' Mr Castle cried. 'You have no reason to be anxious.'

He washed dishes and then
pegged them out to dry.

Not only did he sweep the floors,
he swept the ceilings, too.

He vacuumed the carpets, put the
dough to rise in a warm place …

wiped down the bench, had a
quick cup of tea …

planted a row of cabbages,
folded the washing, baked
the bread *and* a cake …

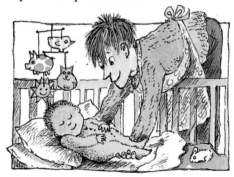

put Carlo down for his
afternoon sleep …

had another cup of tea ...

cleaned the bath ...

prepared dinner ...

read the paper (so as to be well-informed) ...

kissed the children when they came home from school – and Mrs Castle when she came home from work – and asked them all what sort of day they had had.

Then he gave Mrs Castle a glass of sherry, handed her the paper and took the children out for a game on the big green lawn. He was an excellent house-father.

Indeed he was so good that one day he actually ran out of work. While he tried to think of just what to do next there came a soft thud on the roof and then another one.

'Sunspots!' cried Mr Castle and ran outside. But it was not the sound of falling sunspots he had heard, but ripe plums tumbling off the old plum tree which grew behind the house.

Mr Castle was delighted.

'I'll show them,' he cried. 'They think they know all my capacities, but I shall show them talents beyond their wildest dreams.' Gathering up the fallen plums he made three pots of plum jam.

'My dear, how wonderful!' exclaimed Mrs Castle. Clarissa, Clement and Carlo thought it was wonderful, too.

The next day many more plums fell from the tree and Mr Castle made twenty pots of plum jam.

The following day the ground under the tree and much
of the roof were covered with big, purple plums. Mr
Castle made thirty pots of plum jam.

But the day after that there were even more plums and Mr Castle had run out of jam jars.

'What a challenge!' he cried. 'Not a single plum must be wasted.'

He filled all the vases in the house with jam. He filled the glasses they used for sherry. Even Carlo's rabbit mug and the teapot were filled with jam.

'The whole house is like a jam factory,' said Clement.

'It's like a school for jam pots,' said Clarissa.

'Your father is a born artist,' said Mrs Castle. 'He is the Picasso of jam makers.'

'But now we must eat it all up,' said Mr Castle firmly.

They began with jam sandwiches. Mrs Castle, Clement
and Clarissa had jam sandwiches in the lunches Mr Castle
prepared for them every morning. Carlo, who was cutting
new teeth, had jam on his crusts.

'Hooray!' called Mr Castle. 'We've emptied the teapot already. We'll be able to have tea with our scones, pancakes, roly polies and sponge cakes.'

That winter the roof leaked a little. Mr Castle's jam proved very useful, for it stopped leaks as well as being delicious on steamed puddings. When the tile came off the bathroom floor, Mr Castle stuck them down again with jam. After weeks of devoted jam-eating they could put flowers in the vases again and drink sherry from glasses instead of from eggcups.

'I wouldn't care if I never saw another pot of jam in my life,' Clarissa whispered to Clement. 'But don't tell Daddy I said so.'

'You can't help getting sick of jam,' Clement agreed.

In the meantime they had jam with everything, and on everything and under everything. Their dreams became haunted with jam. Clement dreamed that the sky opened and jam rained down on him. Clarissa dreamed of fat shadowy jam pots marching through the night, crying out a terrible war cry of 'Jam! Jam! Jam!'

Mrs Castle dreamed that it was proved that sunspots were caused by too much jam and Carlo dreamed great jammy dreams as well. Their days were full of jam eating and their nights of dreams all dripping with jam.

They even woke up feeling sticky and not in the mood for breakfast (jam on porridge, jam on toast, with a cup of tea sweetened with jam to follow).

Then one morning Mr Castle went to the cupboard to get down the next pot of jam only to find it was empty. There was not a single potful left.

'Let's have egg sandwiches for lunch,' said Mrs Castle.

'Let's have fish and chips,' suggested Clement.

'Spaghetti and salad,' cried Clarissa.

!

'But first let's have a game on the lawn,' said Mr Castle. 'We've eaten so much jam that we look like jam pots ourselves. We shall have to get back to our old shapes.'

While they were playing on the lawn, Mr Castle heard a soft thud on the roof. He looked up at the plum tree enthusiastically. A year of jam eating had gone by.

The plums were ripe again.

Plum Jam

4 lbs of stoned plums
4 lbs of sugar
½ a pint of water.

Simmer the plums
in the water until
soft. Add the sugar
and stir until
dissolved. Boil
until the jam will
set.
Put into clean warm
jars and seal well.